TOLLY GRIMPEN'S TALES OF GROT and HORROR

FEATURING A FREAKY AND FRIGHTENING COLLECTION OF TALES FOR YOUR ENJOYMENT

WRITTEN BY IAN BILLINGS

ILLUSTRATIONS BY HUNT EMERSON

TINY TREE

First Published in 2024 by
Tiny Tree Books
West Wing Studios
Unit 166, The Mall
Luton, LU1 2TL

Text copyright © 2024 Ian Billings
Illustrations copyright © 2024 Hunt Emerson
The moral rights of the author(s) have been asserted.

The right of Ian Billings to be identified as the author of this work has been asserted in accordance with the Copyright, Designs and Patents Act 1988.

All rights reserved. No reproduction, copy or transmission of this publication may be made without express prior written permission. No paragraph of this publication may be reproduced, copied or transmitted except with express prior written permission or in accordance with the provisions of the Copyright Act 1956 (as amended). Any person who commits any unauthorised act in relation to this publication may be liable to criminal prosecution and civil claims for damage.

All characters appearing in this work are fictitious. Any resemblance to real persons, living or dead, is purely coincidental.

BEWARE
ALL WHO ENTER HERE!

(It's Pretty Grotty Inside...)

THE GRUESOME TALE OF THE MUMMY'S NAIL CLIPPINGS

These are "Tolly Grimpen's Tales of Grot and Horror." I am your storyteller, Tolly Grimpen, and this first tale is covered in grot from beginning to end. Please wash your hands after reading it.

This tale begins in England in the year 1893 (before your time). It concerns a girl by the name of Florence Gallop who most considered the greatest explorer in the world in the under-eleven's category. She had explored here, there, and everywhere. Some of over here, a lot of over there and loads of everywhere. In fact, everywhere was where she liked best. She had explored mountains, valleys, forests, rivers, lakes and fields, but one of her most important finds was in a place called Egypt – which is in *that* direction.

Once she discovered her strange discovery (which I'll tell you about in a minute – I'm just building up the tension) she made her way back to Big London and presented it (wait for it…) to the Royal Navigational Society. And this is the speech she gave…

"A Speech of Great Scientific Importance to be Heard by Anyone Interested in Important Things by Florence Gallop. This is a very important speech about nail clippings, so jolly well listen closely and I'll tell you how it all happened.

I have explored lots of the world. I am four feet two inches tall and four feet three inches tall in my hiking boots. I have a large pith helmet and lots of fly-swats. I also have an atlas of the world called *Atlas of the World*, which I use when I go exploring. Being famous and important means I get invited to important places. Once, not long ago, I was asked to explore a lesser part of Egypt (which is in *that* direction) called the Valley of the Baby Camels. I rummaged in that valley until I found the legendary Nail Clippings of Kaki-Tartar. These Clippings had laid amongst other Egyptian artefacts for thousands and thousands of years. I placed them safely in a box and brought them to show you today. The Nail Clippings of Kaki-Tartar, ladies and gentlemen – the eighth wonder of the world. Oh, they've gone!"

The audience were aghast, and no one believed she had actually discovered those ancient nail clippings, but Florence knew what a lot of people didn't know, and what a lot of people didn't know was the Nail Clippings were cursed! Yes, cursed! C...U...R...S...E...D! And they had disappeared! D...I...S...A... (you get the idea...)

Soon the cursed Nail Clippings were wreaking havoc across the whole of London. Soon blackboards were being scraped, peas were being flicked at the poshest of posh restaurants and people found their feet being scratched when there was no one else in the room! It was becoming a slightly Eerie tale, bordering on the Weird, just outside Strange.

The haunted Nail Clippings were scuttling all across London, causing chaos wherever they went. Londoners were aghast (that's twice they've been aghast now) and questions were being asked.

"Who owns those Nail Clippings?"

"What are they going to do next?"

"When will they appear again?"

In fact, the London Times – a very popular newspaper – wrote to Florence Gallop with a very tempting offer.

"Dear Miss Gallop, I am Edwina Scoop of the London Times and I am writing an article about you and your Nail Clippings. Is this whole story a joke, a scam, a scheme? If it is

true then you should be able to produce the Nail Clippings, and if you do we will give you £100,000 in English pound notes."

£100,000 was a lot of money in those days and, indeed, it's a lot of money in these days, too. So, Florence Gallop wrote to Edwina Scoop at the London Times:

"Dearest Miss Scoop, it is not a scam but I can now reveal the Nail Clippings are safely hidden away. I am a serious explorer and I do not do it for profit. I can show you the Nail Clippings but want the money first. I need to buy some new Wellingtons for a forthcoming expedition. And some gloves. Yours sincerely, Florence Gallop (miss)."

Of course, the London Times were not stupid and were not going to give Florence the money without proof.

"We are not stupid – we need proof!" They wrote to her, "Bring the Nail Clippings to the Royal Navigational Society by noon o'clock on Friday and we shall give you the money! All of it! Honest!"

But the question on everyone's lips and ears

was did Florence really have the Nail Clippings or were they still running amok in London? We shall see...

It would be interesting at this point in the story to read the report by Constable Stubble of Scotland Yard about his interview with Florence Gallop.

"I was interviewing Miss Gallop when she revealed to me she had that very night clipped off her own toenails with some nail clippers and put them in a bag. She said only a true expert could tell the difference between her toenails and the Ancient Nail Clippings of Khaki-Tartar."

So, the question on everyone's tongue was what happened next?

Is it a scam?

Is Florence trying to cheat the London Times out of £100,000?

Are the Nail Clippings real?

Are they truly cursed?

The moment Florence burst into the Grand Hall of the society with the bag of toenails in her hand was one they would remember for a very long time. It was Friday at noon and the clock had just stopped its donging. Florence had a mean look in her eye, and the fellows of the society parted like a herd of startled buffalo.

They watched the spectacle unfold.

"I am Florence Gallop! And I have the Nail Clippings of Kaki-Tartar!" she bellowed, and a gaggle of reporters, clutching their pens and papers, crowded around the child, trying to eavesdrop.

"The nail clippings currently running amok in London are not the Nail Clippings of Kaki-Tartar! For they are here!"

And with that, she drew a pouch from her jacket and from it produced ten toenails and laid them on the table. There was a gasp of admiration. The chairman of the Royal Navigational Society was about to make a speech when another voice piped up from the back.

"Stop!" it said, "I am Edwina Scoop of the London Times and those are not the Nail Clippings of Kaki-Tartar."

"Yes, they are!" shouted Florence, "And I claim my £100,000."

"No, they're not!"

The two ladies faced each other head-to-head. Everyone wanted to see what would happen next.

"And I can prove it! In my hand I have a receipt!" Edwina Scoop pulled a tattered slip of paper from her pocket and held it aloft. She continued, "A receipt for a set of nail clippers!"

Another gasp ran around the room, followed

by a confused snort and then an awkward pause. Edwina Scoop stomped up to Florence Gallop and held the receipt before her little face.

"Read what it says!" she ordered.

Gallop gazed at the receipt. She muttered something.

"Speak up!" Scoop ordered, again.

"It says, 'Receipt for One Set of Nail Clippers Purchased by Florence Gallop!'"

Suddenly hundreds of pencils began scribbling on hundreds of note pads and someone far at the back began wittering into one of those new telephone gadgets.

"Now you may be wondering how I came by this receipt?"

The fellows of the society nodded as loudly as they could over the sound of the scribbling pencils.

"I had been corresponding with Florence Gallop in the hope of gaining an interview for my paper, the London Times. One of her replies contained more than just answers to my question. Florence Gallop had accidentally folded this receipt into her letter!"

Constable Stubble of Scotland Yard came into view and strode over to the hub-hub, watching the goings-on that were going-on.

"Constable, arrest that woman!"

Constable Stubble looked about a little nervously and said, "I can't do that, Miss Scoop."

Edwina was clearly not a woman to be tangled with and Stubble was about to get tangled.

"Why not?"

The constable lowered his voice and said, "We ain't got no h'evidence!"

Scoop gestured towards the nail clippings spread out on the table, "This is the evidence!"

Stubble adjusted his tie, polished his whistle and finally wiped his helmet.

"But we don't know they are hers," he said, nodding towards Florence Gallop.

"Ha!" yelped Florence, waving her hat in the air.

"Remove her shoes and socks," replied Scoop softly.

Within seconds Florence was laying on her back on the Grand Banqueting Table in the Grand Hall of the Royal Navigational Society with her socks being tugged from her little feet by a throng of eager journalists and a reluctant policeman.

Florence Gallop's face was frozen in an expression of impending doom. Scoop took the first toenail and held it in the air for all to see. She inspected it closely, nodded sagely and then tried it against Gallop's left big toe. Every pair of eyes in the room stared intently as she did so. It fitted perfectly! One by one each and every toenail on the table was tried against a toe, and one by one every toenail fitted every toe perfectly.

As Constable Stubble stepped forward with his handcuffs, a camera flash went off and the case was proven beyond doubt.

Now, most readers would think that was the end of this particularly grotty tale.

But there is just a little more. Later that night as Florence Gallop, that sad-schemer and dodgy-deceiver, sat alone in the dark cell, a tapping came on the door. It was not a jailer, it was not a policeman, nor a fellow inmate wanting a cup of tea.

Tap, tap, tap it went on the cell door. Over and over all through the night.

Tap, tap, tap.

The tap-tap-tapping of the haunted Nail Clippings of Kaki-Tartar…

THE END

THE SEPTIC TALE OF DOCTOR JEKELL AND MR SHINE

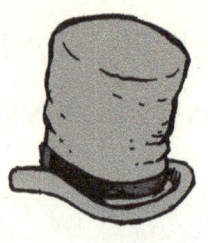

CRASH!!!!

That is the terrifying sound which announces the beginning of this sad story. It is the sound of a stained-glass window, which was once the pride of the Boddlington family, smashing and crashing into thousands of tiny sharp shards. And the smash happened in the middle of the night! Ooooooooooooooooooooooh!

The Boddlingtons had lived at No.1, Snottly Street since 1850 and, upon hearing the shattering, Lord Boddlington wandered from his bed to see what had caused the naughty noise and gazed, bleary-eyed, through the hole.

"What a big hole," he muttered, "about the size of fifty gerbils." Lord Boddlington had a strange way of measuring things. He half expected to find a rogue, but instead he saw something very surprising.

"Slap me with a jellyfish!" he said, as he surveyed the drawing room. He sniffed, he snuffed, he puffed. He didn't know what to say. All his furniture had been re-arranged! Not only that but all the glass had been swept up. Not only that, every nook and cranny was spick and span. His entire house had been cleaned from roof to cellar!

"This is the work of... the most dastardly villain in all of London," he announced to no one in particular, "This is the work of the Phantom Good-Deed-Doer!"

Lord Boddlington gazed through the hole in his window, sighed, sniffed again, hugged his teddy bear and went back to bed.

The home of a much-respected and well-loved doctor, Timothy Jekell, was not far from the Boddlington House and in it was his servant, Sam Sweller, cleaning and polishing the rooms. At that precise moment, the dishevelled and confused doctor burst into the room. His coat was torn, his hat was bent and there was a faint whiff of cleaning fluids about his person. What was Sam to make of all this? Where had his master been till this hour? Sam wondered as he dusted the cat.

Doctor Jekell stumbled into his office, slammed and locked the door then squidged a bit of putty in the keyhole because he knew Sam liked looking through it. Jekell snarled "Ha!" at the doctor's black raven, Edgar, perched on a tottering pile of medical books. "That should keep that pokey-nosed servant's ears out of my business!" And he stuck out his tongue at the door.

"Ha!" snarled Edgar, once more. Only Edgar knew the doctor's secret, and it was a shocking secret of vile villainy. Would you like to hear it? Say, "Yes, please." Thank you. You see, Jekell had been experimenting with the human mind – the good and the evil. He had been trying to separate the two. So far he had only managed to isolate one... and not the one he was expecting.

*

As dawn broke the next day and the sun shone out over a thriving London, Sam Sweller found himself dusting around the laboratory.

"What a to-do last night, eh, Edgar?" said Sam.

"Ha!" said the raven.

"I wonder what that doctor of ours is really up to?" Sam watched, bewildered as the raven started banging his little black beak on a tottering pile of papers.

"What's that, Edgar? You want me to read these papers?" Edgar banged his beak furiously on the pile. "But these are Doctor Jekell's professional notes. I can't read those."

Edgar banged his little beak even more.

"Oh, very well, Edgar, as you insist, but just a sneaky peak." Sam carefully put down his duster and slid a piece of parchment from under Edgar then held it to the light, it read, "The Top-Secret Diary of Doctor Timothy Jekell…"

And Sam started to read.

*

"Extra! Extra! Read all about it!" The paper boy stood on the corner of the hustling, bustling street shouting out the latest blood-curdling headlines, "London Times cries out for justice!"

From out of the shadows slunk Doctor Jekell. He stood and watched the paper boy. "The Phantom Good-Deed-Doer has struck again! Baroness Dribbling-Teabag has had her entire mansion re-decorated whilst on holiday!"

Doctor Jekell stepped towards the boy, menacingly. "Give me a paper!" he snarled.

"That'll be a penny, please, sir," said the boy, handing over a copy.

"I have no money."

"Then I'll have it back," said the boy, grasping for the paper.

"Stay away!" snarled the doctor, who seemed to be doing an awful lot of snarling, "Otherwise…"

and then he produced a beautifully laundered and ironed handkerchief, "I will wipe your nose!"

The boy screamed, "Extra! Extra! Read all about it! Paperboy threatened with cleanly laundered handkerchief in broad daylight! Bravely stands his ground for three seconds then runs off home to his mummy!"

And so, screaming, the boy ran off and Doctor Jekell started to read in the paper of his alter-ego's adventures the previous night.

The next morning the Doctor returned home in a shattered and tattered state. He was confused and splashed with pink emulsion paint. Sam was sitting in the laboratory cupboard pretending to dust a few paperclips. The door was slightly open and Sam, unseen by his master, overheard every word.

"This is the end, Edgar! The end, I say! No more cleaning and dusting and swilling and mopping! No more do-gooding for me! I intend to put a stop to all this, this very day!"

And with those final words, he snapped Sam's mop in two pieces.

"Eeek!" the 'eeek' you just heard came from the mouth of Sam and his mouth, like Sam, was still in the cupboard. Doctor Jekell ripped open the door and stared down at his trembling servant.

"You!" snarled the doctor.

"Me!" said Sam, pointing to himself so they both knew who they were talking about, "I know everything! I have read the diary! I have seen your secret stash of polish and sprays!" Sam drew himself up to his full height, which was not very high and said, "And you broke my mop!"

The Doctor was incensed. He snarled (again) and growled and hissed. Sam, keeping his employer at a distance with one end of the broken mop said, "I shall tell the London Times everything!"

But it was all no use. The Doctor, by far the stronger of the two, overpowered his little odd-job man. He slipped a tin of "Spruce It Up" polish from his waistcoat pocket and held it under Sam's nose as he inhaled it. The room started to wobble and sway and swing and turn inside out, upside down and back to front. The Doctor caught Sam as he fell into a deep, deep sleep. He cackled and snorted and, when he couldn't think of anything else to do, he snarled.

What will happen next?

How will this grotty, snotty tale of naughty good-deed-doer end?

When Sam awoke he found himself sitting in a copper bath. The Doctor stood nearby brandishing hot water and soap.

"This is for my Final Clean," he said, stalking back and forth, waving the soap threateningly, "I am one of the finest scientists in all of London. I have split the human mind in two. I thought I may have isolated the evil side, but no, oh no. I ended up isolating the nice, goodie-goodie part. For the last week my alter-ego, Mr Shine, has been breaking into people's homes across London and..." He could barely bring himself to say the last words, "... cleaning them! If you mutter so much as a single syllable of what you've seen you will be given the biggest, best scrubbing of your life!" He pointed the sponge at Sam and the sunlight glinted off his manic eye. Sam whimpered slightly.

Having secured his odd-job man, the Doctor began concocting a final, huge double dose of do-good-juice. Edgar hopped back and forth on the tottering pile of medical books and watched amazed as his master took a final giddy gulp from the bottle and slowly, very slowly started to transform.

First his ears popped, then his nose straightened with a crack, then his hair grew long and luxurious, then his eyes shimmered until they turned perfect blue, then he turned to his goggle-eyed raven and said, "Call me, Mr Shine!"

Suddenly every possible cleaning implement you could imagine pop-pop-popped into his hands. A bright twinkle danced on his teeth and with a manic cackle he left the house.

*

Constable Stubble of Marlborough Police Station was renowned throughout all of Greater London for being one of the most eagle-eyed coppers ever to blow his whistle on the streets. So it was no surprise then, when Sam entered the police station looking upset, Constable Stubble said, "You are upset!"

In a hurried speech, Sam recounted the horrid events of the last few days. Constable Stubble waved his truncheon in the air and blew his whistle three times he was so excited.

"We must set forth after this vile villain and bring him to justice, and to the police station!" And with those words, Sam and Constable Stubble set off on the trail of the Phantom Good-Deed-Doer!

*

The large chimney at the end of Snottly Street had been pumping out foggy smog and smoggy fog since before anyone could remember – and each plume of smoke had weaved its way into the noses of everyone in London. Before long, Constable Stubble, Sam and Edgar had tracked down the trail of Mr Shine. A slimy line of cleaning fluid had dripped and dribbled and led them to the exact bottom of the belching chimney. They looked up. Tottering on the tip-top was Mr Shine! He stood there looking down defiantly and waving his duster threateningly.

"So I bid farewell to this cruel world," he bellowed. "No more will I slink through the underworld, mopping and dusting and polishing and buffing. This is my Final Tidy!"

And with that cry of victory, he leapt, jumped, hopped and plummeted into the foggy murk of the chimney. Swallowed by the filthy fog.

Constable Stubble and the crowd, which had gathered around, fell as silent as a mushroom. And then a deathly scream was heard. Edgar the raven swooped upwards and into the gaping hole and shortly returned holding only a duster. "Do something, Constable!" shouted Sam.

"I can't, sir, I'm afraid he got clean away..." And the Phantom Good-Deed-Doer was never seen or heard of again.

*

Many months later, at the reading of Doctor Jekell's will, Sam was a little surprised to find all the contents of the house had been left to... Edgar the Raven! Luckily, Edgar kept Sam on as his servant to clean out his birdcage.

THE END

THE BEDRAGGLED TALE OF THE BEWITCHED TEETH

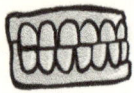

So you want another grotty tale, do you? Then come a little closer and listen.

This grotty, snotty tale begins in a dark and rat-invested prison cell in Highgate, which is a lot of miles in *that* direction. Behind the bolted doors and locked gates sat a man, a prisoner condemned to years in jail for doing something very, very naughty. His withered hair and stubbled face made him look like a confused hedgehog, but he wasn't confused and he certainly wasn't a hedgehog.

"I have a tale to tell!" announced the prisoner as he poked his finger dramatically in the air, startling his cellmate. "A tale to tell of a strange and bizarre incident, which happened to a man called Edmund Dollop." His cellmate nibbled the cheese and listened intently as the prisoner began his tale.

*

Many years ago, Edmund Dollop was known the length and width of the British Empire. He was known through every land under the sun and a few more besides. He was as famous as famous could be and famous for being famous too. He was a hero, an explorer and an adventurer. He was the man who discovered the East Pole. He was the man who had climbed Mount Wibble-Wooo from the inside and he was the man who invented the iron umbrella. And for those achievements he was respected, loved and admired. Until one day something terrible happened. TERRIBLE in capital letters! One day he was visiting Queen Victoria, God bless her little cotton mittens, to receive his one-hundred and ninety-second medal that year. Her Most Gracious Majesty said to him, "Yo, Edders, how's it going? Been to many countries lately and that?"

"Indeed, your noble majesty," Dollop replied and then pronounced the name of the country. It was one of those difficult, awkward names and as he tried to say it he realised his tongue was sticking out of his mouth in front of the noblest of noble queens ever to sit on the throne of Britain.

Chaos erupted! CHAOS with capital letters!

Suddenly, Edmund Dollop was marched from the room.

"Laters, Edders!" shouted the Queen, as her servants started to remove Edmund's medals and then hurled him into the street outside Buckingham Place. Just near the newsagents.

*

For the weeks which followed no one would talk to Edmund Dollop. People scoffed at him in the street, jeered and sometimes poked him with a stick. Soon he could no longer find employment and his great wealth slowly dribbled away. He was destitute. Before long he had to resort to selling all the trinkets and artefacts which he had discovered on his many, many journeys abroad and that is where his final adventure begins…

Amongst the rag-bag of relics in Dollop's keep were the Golden Choppers of the ancient Aztec emperor, Poppocuppacoffeyon, which he unearthed many years ago. But these were no ordinary false teeth. Oh, no. They carried a deadly curse, which Edmund, to his peril, ignored. He leapt from his bed one morning, startling the cat and knocking over his wash basin, grabbed the Golden Choppers, placed them in a bag and headed for Sotheby's. Now you are probably wondering, what is Sotheby's? In fact, why don't you shout out, "What is Sotheby's?" Alright,

alright – don't shout. Sotheby's was and is a great auction house in London where people buy and sell hugely expensive things for stupid prices to show off to guests in their houses.

"Hmmmm, I'm not sure!" said Mr Groop, the valuer who was in charge of valuing things, "I might get seventy-five pounds for it." And then blew his nose loudly.

So, the Golden Choppers of the ancient Aztec emperor, Poppocuppacoffeyon, with the terrible curse were put up for auction.

The day of the sale was dark, dank and stormy and little interest was shown in any of the items for sale. Dollop was starting to worry. If he could not get any money for those choppers he would have nothing left to sell. He gazed across the audience of disinterested faces and his eyes fell on a shadowy figure lurking in the corner, and as the Golden Choppers were announced the shadowy figure began to take interest.

"What am I bid for these lovely Golden Choppers?" asked Mr Groop, expectantly.

No one replied.

"What nothing?"

No one replied, again.

Dollop had to do something. Suddenly he heard himself putting on a funny voice.

"I bid seventy-four pounds!" he shouted.

Mr Groop whooped, "Any more bids?" and the audience suddenly sat up, excited and interested, as the shadowy figure looked about furtively and shouted, "Seventy-five pounds!"

"Sold!" Mr Groop whooped and banged his little hammer. Everyone applauded, but no one was applauding louder than Edmund Dollop. At last, he had some money. At last, he could buy food. At last, he could buy clothes. At last, he could have a shower!

*

Later that day, the pounds were being counted over. "And that's seventy pounds for you and five for us. We don't do this for nothing, you know! Well done, Dollop. You can hold your head up high in society once more."

Edmund Dollop strutted merrily, with one leg in front of the other, down the Strand in London when he stopped outside Madame Julie Verne's Emporium of Clothing. A clothes shop. A very posh and expensive clothes shop.

"Well," thought Dollop, "I have come into a lot of money and I do deserve a treat. I might buy myself a new coat!" The bell tinkled as he stepped through the door and minutes later it was tinkling again as he was thrown out by Madame Julie Verne herself shouting, "Zees is fake money. Do not come into my hugely expensive and beautifully perfumed store with false, fake money. Take your money and go away!"

The shadowy figure who had bought the Golden Choppers of the ancient Aztec emperor, Poppocuppacoffeyon, had paid for them with counterfeit money! False money! Dollop was determined to track him down – but what could he do? The buyer had left no address.

What will happen next?

How will Edmund Dollop get out of the messy mess and become a hero once more?

Who was the shadowy figure?

Will he get his money or his choppers back?

While Edmund Dollop was pondering what to do a newspaper blew down the street, around the corner and slap-bang straight into Edmund's face.

"I've had quite enough bad luck without a newspaper flying into my... but wait – what is this?"

And as he peeled the paper from his face he saw a large advertisement which read "Appearing tonight at the Royal Albert Hall – Opera Sensation, Eva Topsy, who will be singing some of the world's greatest opera arias and showing off her New Golden False Teeth!"

"Golden false teeth?" echoed Dollop and, within seconds, had convinced himself these were the very golden false teeth which had been cheated from him. He must get them back!

He swiftly made his way to the Royal Albert Hall and it wasn't long before he found himself employed as the theatre flyman. He was in charge of the ropes and the pulleys and the levers and the things that go *Twang*! With all his mountaineering experience how could they turn him down? He gazed out at all the equipment under his command and muttered under his breath, "As soon as that opera singer appears I shall make my move!"

Dollop's plan was daring, dangerous and very, very simple. He would wait high above the stage holding a rope. As Eva Topsy started to sing he would judge when her mouth was to be at its widest and then swing down towards her, snatch the teeth from her mouth and then, amidst all the confusion, scuttle off into the night. Well, that was his plan. What happened was slightly different...

*

The night of the performance came. It was a glittering event. Dukes, earls, counts, dames and duchesses drew up in horse-drawn carriages and waved happily as they made their way to their seats.

And then the main guest arrived. The audience *ooohed* and *ahhhed* and fluttered their fans as Queen Victoria appeared in the royal box, gave a thumbs up and shouted, "How's it going, dudes?" Everyone giggled politely as the lights dimmed.

High above the stage Edmund Dollop stood holding the rope in his trembling hand and, with bated breath, waited for the precise moment when he could strike.

A drum roll began, the overture tumbled loudly and brightly from the orchestra pit and thirty of the world's greatest musicians beat and stroke and blew and plucked some of the most beautiful music to enter the ears of the crowded audience. Even Queen Victoria stopped eating her popcorn long enough to shout, "S'alright, innit!"

Once, twice and then three times Eva Topsy hit a high note and opened her mouth widely, displaying the golden false teeth.

"But not widely enough," thought Dollop, "Next time…"

Two, three, four more arias were sung but Dollop still waited.

Eva Topsy then announced her final song.

There was silence (which was spoiled slightly by Queen Victoria's snoring) and then the orchestra erupted with the most stunning music ever heard and Eva Topsy prepared to sing.

But she didn't sing. Oh, no. Instead from out of her mouth came a strange war chant. A haunting and bewitching sound which confused and bewildered the audience and frightened Eva Topsy who was pointing frantically at her teeth as the sound emerged.

What were they to do?

The sound droned on as the conductor jumped from the orchestra pit and tried to dislodge the teeth with his baton but failed. Next, a long piece of string was attached to the teeth and the entire orchestra gathered to tug at it.

The audience looked on almost hypnotised by the sight as suddenly, and with a loud pop, the teeth flew from Eva's mouth and, still attached to the string, swung wildly across the auditorium slapping the faces of all the dukes and duchesses in the front row.

Edmund was as bewildered as everyone, but suddenly looked at the conductor and recognised him as...

"The shadowy figure at Sotheby's!"

Dollop shrieked in surprise, lost grip of his rope, fell from the top of the theatre, hit a big drum and with a loud *bo-ing* bounced into the auditorium where he was chased up the aisle by two policemen and an ice-cream seller and disappeared into the night. They chased him along the roof of the Albert Hall. Finally, they caught him, arrested him and threw him in jail. The charge? Teeth smuggling.

Sadly, the teeth were never found and it was assumed they had fallen in the River Thames. But they hadn't...

The prisoner, who began our tale, sat in his cell and turned to his cellmate who finished his cheese, squeaked in delight and waved his tail. Then the prisoner stood and loudly declared...

"This is a true tale, for I am the hero of it; I am Edmund Dollop and these are my Golden Teeth!"

And then he smiled broadly, the sunlight glinted off his choppers and his mouse cellmate clapped his little paws.

THE END

THE RANCID TALE OF THE CHILD PHENOMENON

You really are a glutton for grot, aren't you? Very well, if you can stand another tale, here it is…

Clickety clop, clickety clop, clickety clop. Three surprisingly large horses came down Pall Mall in London sometime in the late 1880's followed by a grumpy donkey and two very confused chickens. You may think this an odd sight. Indeed, but what was an even odder sight was they were pulling ten large caravans and from each was festooned lots of bunting, flags and banners. Wherever was it going? Whatever had arrived in London Town? Well, I shall tell you.

This was Doctor Blackwood's Carnival of the Bizarre! It was known the length and breadth of England as the most impressive, notorious and outright weird carnival ever to tour the country. This was the carnival which boasted the time-travelling mole, the hiccupping chicken and the tap-dancing llama. But not only animals – there were humans, too. The astounding Mrs Flopping who could lick her ear with her tongue, the

Amazing Tweak whose knees could sing opera and The Grand Vizier of Tonk who could juggle soil. Wherever and whenever Doctor Blackwood's Carnival of the Bizarre appeared people would turn out in their droves and in London Town there were a lot of droves turning out.

Without any announcement, and simply by word of mouth and the wagging tongues of London people, the Carnival (which had pitched itself in a quiet corner of Hyde Park) was soon awash with inquisitive nosey folk all eager to see what secrets and surprises lay behind those canvas tents. And all paying lots of money to do so.

But all was not well in Doctor Blackwood's Carnival of the Bizarre. Oh, no. For Doctor Blackwood, a horrid, grotty man with angry eyebrows and an even angrier nose was locked in a caravan and engaged in an argument with a sword-swallower called Bertie Pinch.

"But I can't face another sword, boss," pleaded Bertie, "they give me indigestion."

Blackwood snarled his most snarly snarl, "I get lots of money from people wanting to see you swallow swords. It's a carnival classic. Get out there and start swallowing!"

"I could do a couple of paper clips and a toothpick!" offered Bertie.

"Swords or you're sacked!" bellowed Blackwood, slamming the caravan door as he left.

Bertie pondered his fate. Whatever was he to do? However could he make money? He needed to think of something and think of it quickly. Unfortunately, quick thinking was not what Bertie Pinch did best. What he did best was swallow swords and he could no longer do that. He needed something – or someone – to help him make money.

"Morning, Daddy!" the voice came from the mouth of Bertie's eldest and only son, Little Bert. "Do you want a cup of tea? No, wait, you want a cup of coffee. And you want some bacon and egg on toast."

"Stop reading my mind!" shouted his father, "I'm trying to think."

"I know you are. I read your mind. You are trying to think of a way to make some money for your boss because you can no longer swallow swords."

"I know!"

"I know you know," smiled Little Bert.

"Stop reading my mind and put the kettle on!"

Little Bert had been born and brought up in the carnival and, being surrounded by strange and weird people and animals, he thought nothing of his own unique talent. He could read minds. He read them all the time. He knew loads about all the people in the carnival and all the people who visited. He knew a lot about the secret life of the chickens, too.

"How many fingers am I holding up?" his father suddenly said in the flickering candlelight.

"Two, three, two, four, five. Stop changing your fingers!" said Little Bert.

He was right – his father kept changing his fingers. Then Little Bert said, "I know what you are thinking."

"You always know what I'm thinking, Bert boy. So, what am I thinking right now?"

His son looked up into the eyes of his father and said, "You're thinking how you could use my special talent to make some money for your boss and maybe make some for yourself as well."

"That's right, Bert boy! And it's time to start your training!" and he slowly closed the door of the caravan with a creak.

"Extra! Extra! Read all about it. New attraction announced at Doctor Blackwood's Carnival of the Bizarre. Mind-reading boy will read your mind and the mind of your pet for three shillings. It's a bargain!"

The paperboy strutted up and down Hyde Park barking out the headlines in the paper, which were all about the carnival. It was not long before hundreds and hundreds of people rolled up wanting to see the Child Phenomenon. His first performance proved a huge success. Before a thronging crowd of paying people, he correctly guessed which card Mrs Blenkinsop had chosen (and where she had hidden it) and correctly guessed the first ten names of Rev. Flannel's eldest child. Before long, word had got around London and everyone wanted a private mind-reading from Little Bertie.

"Extra! Extra! Read all about it! The Child Phenomenon proves himself a great success in Hyde Park. Offers private mind-reading sessions. And today's lucky bingo numbers!"

And riding on the success of the previous night Little Bert, under the watchful eye of his father who was under the watchful eye of Doctor Blackwood, started private mind-reading sessions, but it did not go well.

First, he misread Mrs Arkwright's mind and told her that her favourite hat was made of custard, then he misread Mr Ripley's mind and told him his favourite colour was blue (when the whole city knew it was red) and he misread Mrs Jupiter's mind when he told her she didn't like gooseberries when she did! Before long everyone was asking for their money back. Shilling by shilling throughout the day was returned to the people who had paid hugely to have their minds read. Bertie Pinch was beside himself with anger, and beside him with even more anger was Doctor Blackwood.

But what happens next?

How will Bertie Pinch make money?

Will he be thrown out of the carnival?

Will Little Bert go with him?

What will become of the Pinch family?

*

It was midnight in Doctor Blackwood's Carnival of the Bizarre and the llamas were snuggled up under their duvets, the chickens were finishing their bird seed and a stranger was scurrying across Hyde Park by moonlight. The shadowy figure tip-toed across to Bertie Pinch's tent and knocked on the flap, but it was canvas and didn't knock. They tried again. Nope, no use.

"Knock, knock, knock!" said the voice of the shadowy figure. The flap was pulled back and out peered the tired and bewildered face of Bertie Pinch who had just woken from a deep sleep.

"Wossup?" he rubbed his eyes and tried to focus on the visitor. And slowly, very, very slowly the visitor came into focus and Bertie was overwhelmed by what, and by who, he saw.

"Your majesty!" he said and saluted, then remembered he wasn't a soldier and stopped saluting and started bowing. He bowed three times then stopped and curtseyed twice.

It was not a dream. It was not an apparition. It was Her Royal Highness, Her Majesty, Queen Victoria the First of Buckingham Palace and England and Empress of All of India and a Bit of Africa.

"Pinch, dude! What's happening, man?" The Queen surprised him with a vigorous high-five and then clicked her fingers. From out of the darkness a royal servant arrived carrying what appeared to be an empty goldfish bowl.

"Empty!" said the Queen, "Gone. My fish. Well gone. I used to love my fish. He was the only one what really understood me. I miss him so much. I'm well sad. Look at my face. If only I could speak to my Oswald just one more time. I can pay handsomely!"

Bertie looked about. He was a bit confused, and he had a lot to be confused about. Why was the most famous monarch in the history of the world standing outside his tent with an empty goldfish bowl?

"I want your child phenomenon to contact my fish."

That was why! A thousand thoughts tumbled through Bertie's naughty brain. Is this the way to make more money than he could dream of? Could he become a squillionaire just in one night?

"What sort of money are we talking, Maj?" and he curtseyed again.

"Two million pounds!"

Within seconds Bertie was at his son's bed. He pulled back the sheets and revealed – an empty bed! Bertie was beside himself with anger and confusion. He rushed back to the waiting queen.

"Slight problem, Maj," he curtseyed, "The boy who does the readings has gone."

"Gone?"

"Gone! I could have a go myself if you like?"

But Her Majesty didn't like. She turned on her heels and handed back the bowl to her servant who tutted angrily at Bert as they both strode off into the night.

Where was his son? He was on the cusp of making mountains of money and his son had legged it. He must be found.

That night Bertie and his carnival friends scoured London in search of the lost child. There were llamas, moles and chickens all over London – yet none could find Little Bert.

Then, as they regrouped and caught their breath by a tavern, they heard a voice within. A voice they recognised.

"I predict your next card will be the seven of diamonds."

"Correct!"

Then there was a cheer. Bertie peered in through an open window and there was his son surrounded by piles of shillings and surrounding the piles of shillings were lots of people – all betting he could not guess the next card. And he could!

"He's got his powers back!" whooped Bertie as he swiftly ran into the tavern, grabbed his son, curtseyed to the guests and made off with him over his shoulder instructing the llamas to collect the money as he fled.

"Do you have an appointment?" asked the guard at Buckingham Place.

"I am Bertie Pinch and this is my mind-reading son. Her Majesty wants to see us to make contact with her dead fish."

"Well, there's nothing on the list. Are you sure you are psychic?"

Little Bert suddenly said, "You are wearing blue pants with yellow spots!"

The guard threw open the gate and whispered, "Keep that to yourselves, please. Her Majesty is in the dining room."

Her Majesty greeted the pair with two enthusiastic high-fives and a couple of fist-bumps, cracked open a bottle of lemonade and said, "Impress me, dudes, and that pile of dosh is yours!" And she gestured towards a massive pile of money sitting on a table.

Before long all the curtains in the room were drawn, a single candle flickered on the dining table and Bertie, his son and the Queen were huddled around the empty fish bowl.

"Oswald are you there?" asked Little Bert, and then he changed his voice, "Yes, I am here. What do you wish of me?"

At which point his father suddenly howled in pain, "I got candle wax on my finger!"

"Well, go and wash it off!" ordered the Queen, and one of her servants showed him to the nearest bathroom.

Without him, Queen Victoria and the Child Phenomenon started receiving messages from the dead fish (it was actually Little Bert faking it, but Her Majesty was completely convinced).

"I have missed you, Oswald!" said the Queen, dabbing her tears with a royal hanky.

"I have missed you, too!" said Bert, in his fish voice, "I haven't seen you since Thursday…"

"Friday!" corrected the queen.

"Yes, that's what I mean – Friday!"

Then Her Majesty said, "Dude, do me a favour. Could you make Oswald appear?"

And that is when things got really interesting. Little Bert had never made anything materialise out of nowhere before, but he was convinced he could do it. He closed his eyes. He hummed quietly then strained loudly. And then there was a loud pop. But it did not seem to come from the room they were in. Then he said, "I think I've done it."

"But the bowl is still empty, dude!" said the Queen, swilling the water.

"So, if he hasn't appeared in the bowl," said Little Bert, "He must have appeared in another source of water. Where is the nearest source of water?"

"The lav," announced Her Majesty, "Where the dad dude just went to wash his hands."

"Then Oswald the goldfish has materialised in your lavatory sink, your Majesty!"

"Goldfish? I never said Oswald was a goldfish," said the Queen.

"Then what was he?" asked Little Bert.

"Piranha!"

And just as she said that Bertie Pinch ran into the room shouting, "I just bent down to wash my face and there it was!"

The Queen and Little Bert turned around to see what "that" was and "that" was a huge green piranha fish biting Bertie's nose.

"Ooooooooooooooo!!!"

They prised it off and plopped it in the bowl.

"Oswald!" shrieked the Queen in delight and gazed into the water. The fish gazed back.

Very quietly Bert and Little Bert gathered together all the money and slowly and quietly disappeared into the night. And they never returned to Doctor Blackwood's Carnival of the Bizarre ever again.

THE END

THE SCABBY TALE OF THE GHOULISH GRAMOPHONE

So you dared turn another page did you? Well, keep this particular page at arm's length – it's very, very grotty.

Cyrus Phelps was, without doubt, the most urchinest of urchins ever to scuttle the streets of London. He made his money nicking, robbing, stealing, thieving, plundering, ransacking and generally helping himself to things which he had no business helping himself to. Like sherbet. He loved sherbet. He couldn't get enough of it. He once tried to get more than enough from *Mrs Bracket's Candy Emporium*, but Mrs Bracket was having no nicking in her store and regularly chased Cyrus off the premises with a very large stick of rock – "Get out of my emporium!"

After one very long day of nicking, in which Cyrus had managed to thieve nothing other than a small comb, two pebbles and a handful of sherbet, he was walking (scuttling more like) down a road when he saw a woman fighting with an angry octopus. Cyrus couldn't believe his eyes. He rubbed them just to make sure, but that was what he saw and what he heard was horrid. It was a squawking, squalling, droning noise – like an angry octopus. Only it wasn't an angry octopus and the woman wasn't fighting it, but at this point Cyrus didn't know that. He lurched towards the woman and tried pulling the octopus from her. She seemed reluctant to let it go. Cyrus tugged again and the woman started shouting, "Unhand me, you ruffian!" But Cyrus was not going to unhand her and tugged and tugged and tugged until, with a loud wrench, he separated the woman from her octopus.

And then he realised it was not an octopus.

"Give me back my bagpipes!" shouted the woman, snatching them off Cyrus.

"I'm sorry, lady, I thought you was being attacked!"

"Well, I'm not, you doofus!" and she started playing them again. Well, I say play, but it sounded like the worst sound you could ever imagine. Cyrus wondered why she was doing it.

"Why are you doing that?" he asked.

"Because music is the most beautiful sound in the world!" And continued making the bagpipes squeal again.

"I want to do that one day," Cyrus heard himself saying.

The woman suddenly stopped mid-squeal and looked at Cyrus, "Do you?"

"I do!" said Cyrus, and that is the moment his life changed.

Mrs Skrint (as the woman later introduced herself) was impressed by Cyrus's ambition and promised to help him. You see she worked in Harrods' Music Department (Harrods is a big shop in London round the corner from the Tower of London) and so was very well placed to get Cyrus involved in the world of music. He started off in a very small way though. He was appointed under-under-under-stairs boy in the new Gramophone Department.

What is a gramophone you may be asking. You may be asking what is for lunch, or you may be asking what's that on my shoe? I don't know what you are asking, because I cannot hear you so I'm going to guess you are asking what is a gramophone? Well, I'll tell you. In the olden days, when this story is set, music could only be played through pianos, trumpets or, if you were very unlucky, bagpipes. But a new invention had recently been invented and it was called a gramophone, which was a machine for playing music. You put a flat disk on a turntable, wound it up and put a needle on the rotating disk, and out of a large horn came music. All sorts of music. Soft music, loud music, fast music, slow music, happy music, sad music. Every sort of music.

And from the very first moment Cyrus saw a gramophone he became besotted – and promised himself one day to be on a record somehow. He looked around the dark cupboard where he was working and thought, "It'll be a long time before that happens, though."

Eighteen hours Cyrus spent each day cleaning the holes of the records and making the bags to put them in. All to earn a penny a week. A penny! That is almost worth a penny! It was probably the dullest of all the dull jobs in the world. Over and over and over he did the same thing, but in the back of his mind was one dream – to be on a record!

One day Cyrus smuggled in a little bag of sherbet, which he kept dipping his finger into behind Mrs Skrint's back. Every time she turned away she heard a loud slurp and when she turned back to look at Cyrus he was looking very innocent and very busy. But, by accident, then Cyrus inhaled some sherbet very loudly; Mrs Skrint whizzed around and Cyrus couldn't control himself.

"Ah!"

"Whatever is happening, Cyrus?"
"Ah!"
"You are covered in sherbet!"
"Ah!"
"Please tell me you are not about to…"
"Choooooooooooooo!"

Cyrus sneezed on Mrs Skrint. It was snotty. It was grotty. It was gross!

Mrs Skrint wiped her face in disbelief and bellowed, "Get out of my shop! Never return and take your sherbet with you, you doofus!"

Two burly guards marched Cyrus from his cupboard and threw him out on the street where he landed in the wettest puddle you could imagine.

Plop!

Cyrus's ambition was thwarted. He would never appear on a gramophone record. He would never have his dream come true and it was all over – or was it?

"I shall wreak a terrible revenge!" hissed Cyrus as he sat in the puddle, "I shall cause havoc and mayhem for Mrs Skrint. No one treats Cyrus Phelps like this!"

He leapt to his feet in the puddle and a horse-drawn carriage drove passed and splashed water all over him.

But what will happen next?

What will be Cyrus's terrible revenge?

What will be the havoc and the mayhem?

How will it all end?

Well, I'll tell you what happens next. Take your fingers out of your ears and listen! That very night – the night after the incident in Harrods with the sherbet and the puddle – Cyrus Phelps broke back into the store from which he had previously been sacked. Yes, broke back in! You read that correctly. There was a wobbly door which Cyrus knew about and with the right amount of pushing and shoving it could be opened, and with the right amount of pushing and shoving Cyrus opened it – and crept in.

But why was Cyrus there, you may be asking. What was he doing? Was he up to no good? Well, if you just stopped asking questions I could tell you. Cyrus was a bad-deed-doer and he was on course to do the baddest deed in his bad-deed-doing career.

Lit by the twinkling moonlight, right in the centre of the store, under a huge glass dome sat the object Cyrus was looking for. With a candle flickering nervously in his fist he crept closer. This was the brand new, state-of-the-art gramophone! It was made of burnished oak wood with golden knobs and golden handles and the biggest, widest horn you could ever see. It cost five shillings! An unimaginable amount of money, but Cyrus imagined it and he wanted it!

Very carefully and very cautiously Cyrus slipped the grand gramophone from under the glass dome, hid it under his jumper and ran off into the night.

The next day Cyrus was sitting in his mouldy room on his mouldy bed looking at the Grand Gramophone on a mouldy table when a knock came knocking at the door, as knocks do.

"Knock, knock, knock!"

It was Miss Gently, his landlady, who was nothing like her name. I mean, she was a landlady, but she did not do things gently. This became clear to Cyrus when the door swung open on its creaking hinges and Miss Gently was silhouetted in the candlelight.

"Where's my rent, fish face?" she shouted, scanning the room. Luckily Cyrus had covered the gramophone with his mouldy shirt so she didn't see it. What she did see, though, was Cyrus's confused and innocent-looking face.

"Oh, please, please, please, sweet Miss Gently. I have no job and I have no money to pay the rent, please do not throw me out into the cold, cold snow."

"It's July, fish face. Get your things!"

But Cyrus was not to be thwarted. Oh, no! He swiftly pulled off the shirt and pointed dramatically at the Gramophone. Miss Gently was shocked.

"That's the brand new, state-of-the-art gramophone! Made of burnished oak wood with golden knobs and golden handles and the biggest, widest horn I ever saw!" she said, in awe.

"The very one!" snarled Cyrus and slipped a disk onto the turntable, wound it up and placed the needle on it.

Within seconds Miss Gently was entranced with the beautiful and beguiling sounds coming from the gramophone. It was the most beautiful sound ever, ever! She started dancing gently (for once) around the room, humming to herself.

But then Cyrus did a very naughty thing. He started to speed up the gramophone. He made it play faster and faster and faster – until the music was just one big painful noise making Miss Gently scream loudly and run from the room.

"Gosh!" thought Cyrus, slowing down the record, "If that's the effect it has on Miss Gently, then imagine the effect it would have on the evil Mrs Skrint!"

Before long Cyrus found himself pushing and shoving on the wobbly door leading to Harrods. He slipped through with the gramophone beneath his jumper and hid, undetected, in a hidey-hole in the wall of Mrs Skrint's office. As soon as she arrived Cyrus started to play a record and, like Miss Gently, Mrs Skrint became entranced and started waltzing around the room, but then Cyrus did a naughty deed and started, once more, to speed up the record until it was a horrid din. Mrs Skrint howled like a walrus and jumped through the window. Luckily, it was a ground-floor window and Cyrus could see her running up the street, screaming and holding her ears.

Realising the power of the gramophone, Cyrus Phelps' mind was consumed by thoughts of further naughty deeds. Now he can get revenge on every person who had ever done him wrong – every person who poked him or kicked him or stole his sherbet. Now was his chance to get even with the world!

Over the next few weeks Cyrus went mad avenging everyone who had ever upset him – and quite a few who had not. London was awash with gossip about the latest fiendish deed. A headline in the Times read, "The Ghoulish Gramophone – Is it a Wind-up?"

For days Cyrus pursued his enemies, little knowing his vile ambition was leading him to a sorry end.

After a few days of getting over her madness, Mrs Skrint tried to take her job back at Harrods but was rejected. She was so incensed she became determined to uncover the truth behind the Ghoulish Gramophone.

While sniffing around the scene of the latest Gramophone Crime, Mrs Skrint discovered a clue – a small pile of sherbet. Who did she know who liked sherbet? She tried to think…

"Knock, knock, knock."

The knocking came on the door of Cyrus's mouldy apartment. He hugged the gramophone closer and shouted, "Go away Miss Gently – I owe you nothing!"

The door opened with the creakiest of creaks and standing silhouetted was not Miss Gently; it was Mrs Skrint! Cyrus whooped with surprise and leapt out the window, taking the Ghoulish Gramophone with him. But what he didn't realise was he was leaving a trail of sherbet behind him – it was trickling out a hole in his pocket!

It didn't take Mrs Skrint long to track down the trail of sherbet and the person who owned it to the Official Harrods Record Pressing Company. It was the place where they made the actual records in big smashing, crashing presses – it was a very, very dangerous place. Oh, yes. And tottering high on a wall above it all Mrs Skrint saw Cyrus, holding the Ghoulish Gramophone!

"Come one step nearer and see what happens!" he shouted, and so Mrs Skrint took one step nearer.

"What happens?" she shouted up at him.

"I'm not sure," shouted Cyrus back, "I'll have some sherbet and a think."

He pulled a handful of sherbet from his pocket and stuffed it in his angry mouth. A lot of it missed his mouth, fell on the wall and formed a slippy, sloppy mess. A very slippy, sloppy mess…

Suddenly Cyrus pointed his finger in the air and announced, "This is what I shall do next…"

And what he did next was not what he intended to do next. What he did next was shout, "Ooooooops!" then slipped in the slippy, sloppy mess of sherbet and fell and fell and fell…

But where he landed no one really knew, for he was never found. Some say he landed safely and ran off into the night. Some say he met a far, far worse fate. But all that we know is Cyrus Phelps, the urchinest of urchins, was no more.

*

A month or so later a press conference was arranged and Mrs Skrint described the events of that ominous night.

"And he fell and he fell and he fell..." she concluded.

"But where?" asked a reporter.

Mrs Skrint winked at them all, produced a record, and put it on. The gramophone started to play beautiful, beguiling music which enchanted all the reporters and just before they all started to get up to dance the music faded and all they heard was a tiny, but familiar voice, saying...

"Help me! I'm stuck, stuck, stuck, stuck, stuck, stuck, stuck, stuck, stuck, stuck, stuck, stuck, stuck..."

THE END

THE FESTERING TALE OF UNCLE CLODD

For my final grotty tale in this grotty collection I turn to one Betsy Pollett, a girl of about ten years old, whose sensational diary fell into my hands some years ago.

Our tale begins in a dark room of a dark house in a dark alley one dark night when Betsy was pulling the tattered bedsheet up to her nose and staring out at the slightly dark moon. She dreamed of happy days, of sweet merry times, of friendships and joy, and of days that were not so dark. But her days were dark, and mainly because of her mother.

CRASH! The door to her pokey bedroom crashed open and in stomped her mother, who was not a nice lady.

"I am not a nice lady!" she shrieked. See? I told you, "And I'm fed up with you laying there dreaming of happy days, merry times, friendship and joy. It's time you stood on your own two feet!"

Betsy looked at her own two feet poking out from under the sheet and wondered what her mother meant.

"What I mean is I'm sending you away!"

Betsy was about to squeal, "Please don't send me away," but thought the place she was being sent to might be better than the place she was currently in.

"Consider it a treat! You're going to stay with Strange Uncle Byron."

"Not Strange Uncle Byron," moaned Betsy and the candle shivered as she spoke.

"Yes, Strange Uncle Byron!" whooped her mother.

"But when shall I be leaving?"

A knock came to the door downstairs.

"Did somebody order a horse-drawn carriage?" shouted a voice below.

Betsy's mother smiled a cruel smile, "About nowish."

Strange Uncle Byron, who was tall, skinny and very pale, lived in a tattered, battered and really ram-shackled mansion on the edge of the cliffs overlooking the North Sea – which is in *that* direction. He was a secretive man and though not unkind, far from friendly.

"Take your bags and clutter and stick them in your room then leave me alone." Strange Uncle Byron announced as the coach driver deposited Betsy on his doorstep a few hours later. Then he flittered away in the dusty darkness. Betsy sighed and looked out of the window at the cold, cold sea.

Strange Uncle Byron's days were spent pottering around and running errands, about which he said very little. He had no time for his niece who soon became very, very, very bored and began exploring the mansion.

One afternoon, while rummaging in the library, Betsy met Eileen, Strange Uncle Byron's chambermaid.

"Afternoon, ma'am." Eileen curtseyed a deep curtsey.

"Don't you remove your hat when addressing your betters?" asked Betsy. Eileen was wearing a top hat indoors, which Betsy thought not only odd but a little rude.

Eileen touched her top hat and said nervously, "I never removes me hat, miss. Not never no," and with that she scuttled out of the room, dusting a few things as she went.

Betsy thought this was very odd behaviour, but living in an odd house with an odd uncle it didn't surprise her the chambermaid would be odd too, but she was VERY odd – with capital letters!

As the hours grew into days and days grew into weeks Betsy started to befriend Eileen and found they had a common interest in worms, puddle water and chickens. Soon the friendship was blossoming as each day they went looking for worms, or chickens, or puddles.

But then, one dark night, a dark storm shook the dark mansion, dislodging generations of dust. Betsy awoke to ask her uncle what was occurring, but Strange Uncle Bryon was nowhere to be seen. She looked in every room, but he was nowhere to be seen again. Soon Betsy sought comfort with her new friend, Eileen. Huddling and cuddling each other they looked out of the highest window at the stormy night. Below the battered, tattered mansion the roads were flooded and impassable.

"No one can get in…" said Betsy softly.

"And no one can get out…" said Eileen, even more softly.

CRACK! A crack of thunder exploded overhead as cracks of thunder tend to do and Betsy and Eileen went scurrying for cover under the bed. And as Betsy pulled Eileen to safety the chambermaid's hat was knocked off.

"What's that?" asked Betsy, pointing to a small lump on Eileen's head.

"Nuffin'," said Eileen, grabbing her hat.

"But it just sniffed!"

"It didn't!"

"It just sniffed again!"

"Didn't!"

"Eileen, do you have an extra nose on top of your head?"

"I don't want to talk about it!" said Eileen, slamming the hat on her head and pulling a face.

Betsy stared out from under the bed at the storm. Why has Eileen got an extra nose, she thought, and more importantly, how did it get there?

The next morning the storm cleared and Betsy came to breakfast. Just as she was tucking into her cornflakes, Strange Uncle Byron appeared and said, "Betsy, allow me to introduce Uncle Clodd," and with those words, he opened the door to the cellar and out stepped a big, thick-set man with dark staring eyes, stitches across his forehead and what looked like bolts in his neck.

Betsy was bewildered. How had this man got into the mansion if all the roads last night were impassable?

Who was he?

What was he here to do?

Why had he got stitches in his forehead?

And why had he got bolts in his neck?

*

Over the next few days, Betsy tried to unravel the story of this Uncle Clodd, and also the story of

Eileen's nose. Day by day she watched Uncle Clodd closely. Very closely indeed. She watched every move, every gesture, every shrug, every expression and she started making notes in her diary.

"Uncle Clodd is very odd! It is almost like he has different personalities. He behaves in five very distinctly different ways. His legs are dexterous like a ballet dancer's, one arm is muscular like a sailor's but the other is thin and weak; the fingers keep dipping into places they shouldn't. His torso seems old and fat like an ale drinker, whilst his head is as tiny as an old lady's. And Uncle Clodd spends his days walking around and around the mansion opening and closing his mouth. I wonder why?"

One cold night as Strange Uncle Byron, Uncle Clodd and Betsy were sitting down to dinner a knock came to the door.

Strange Uncle Byron grabbed all the cutlery and held it to his chest.

"Who can that be at this hour?" he said as his face turned red.

"There is only one way to find out," said Betsy, jumping off her chair and passing Uncle Clodd who was opening and closing his mouth.

Standing in the doorway was a small man in a raincoat who was showing her a badge, "I am

Inspector End of the Yard. And I am in pursuit of five missing people." He stepped into the room uninvited. Strange Uncle Byron dropped all the cutlery and Uncle Clodd just kept opening and closing his mouth.

Inspector End of the Yard pulled out a magnifying glass and inspected a few things with it because that's what inspectors do and where they get their name. He suddenly stopped inspecting things and announced, "Five people have recently gone missing in the vicinity and I was wondering if any of you knew of their whereabouts."

Strange Uncle Byron started picking up the cutlery muttering, "I don't know anything about anything, I'm afraid. I don't get out much."

Uncle Clodd quietly opened and closed his mouth.

Then Betsy said, "Who are they?"

Inspector End of the Yard placed five photographs on the dining table:

A ballet dancer.

A sailor.

A pickpocket.

A landlord.

An old lady.

"I have never seen them before in my life!" shrieked Strange Uncle Byron, "And neither have

Uncle Clodd or Betsy!" He quickly gathered the photographs, handed them back to the inspector and started ushering him out of the house.

"Oh, and by the way, you haven't seen my goldfish, have you?" said the inspector, but no more was heard as Strange Uncle Byron slammed the door in his face.

The next day Betsy, who was becoming more and more intrigued by this mystery, set about solving the riddle of her uncle's strange behaviour. Whatever does he get up to? And where does he get up to it? Walking down a corridor Betsy saw Eileen cleaning a doorknob to a room she had never entered.

"What's in there, Eileen?"

"Nuffin', miss."

"There must be something. I've never been in there. I think I shall go and look!"

And before Eileen could stop her, Betsy had opened the door, stepped in and what she saw amazed her. Test tubes bubbled and babbled, flasks of strange liquid gurgled and puffs of steaming mist hung in the air.

"It's a laboratory!" Betsy announced.

"Is it?" said Eileen, "I never noticed." And a sniff came from under her hat. Suddenly everything became clear to Betsy and she fled from the room and started scribbling her thoughts in her diary.

"Uncle Byron has constructed Uncle Clodd from all the missing people and fiendishly brought them back to life. Yuck! What a dastardly deed!" she wrote.

The next morning at breakfast, Betsy watched carefully as Uncle Clodd's right hand tried to slip a spoon into his pocket, but then his left hand slapped it for being naughty. Two different personalities, Betsy thought, I must be right. Later that day she took Uncle Clodd aside while Strange Uncle Byron was not around and explained to him what had happened. His mouth kept opening and closing faster and faster. And, before she knew it, Uncle Clodd had leapt upstairs to Strange Uncle Byron's laboratory and Betsy and Eileen huddled in the kitchen while they heard grunts and groans and moans and crashes and smashes.

Suddenly a ladder appeared at the window outside and, as they peered out, they saw Strange Uncle Byron climbing down it pursued by a very angry Uncle Clodd. They both leapt off the ladder and into the garden. Strange Uncle Byron running away, followed by a wailing Uncle Clodd.

Now what happened next is lost in the mists of time, but some folk say Uncle Clodd chased

Strange Uncle Byron onto a ship, which sailed out to sea and they spent their last days running around the deck chasing each other. They say it disappeared over the horizon. That is what *they* said, but you know what *they* are like. Perhaps that is what happened. Perhaps we should leave them chasing each other forever and ever.

And as for the lost goldfish. Well, did you notice Uncle Clodd kept opening and closing his mouth? That was because Strange Uncle Byron had given him the brain of the goldfish!

But what happened to Betsy and Eileen you're probably asking? Well, they stayed in the mansion together for the rest of their lives and never, ever spoke of the strange event of Strange Uncle Byron and Uncle Clodd ever again.

THE END

You made it to the back of the book... I am impressed!

I never expected you to make it this far, through all the revolting grot and horror, but here you are.

Well, I must thank you for reading these tales; a gift perhaps?

Turn the page if you dare and see a new side to the characters found in this tome. Take a peek and see if there is anything new you can pick out.

FAREWELL!

THE GRUESOME TALE OF THE MUMMY'S NAIL CLIPPINGS

THE SEPTIC TALE OF DOCTOR JEKELL AND MR SHINE

THE BEDRAGGLED TALE OF THE BEWITCHED TEETH

THE RANCID TALE OF THE CHILD PHENOMENON

THE SCABBY TALE OF
THE GHOULISH GRAMOPHONE

THE FESTERING TALE OF UNCLE CLODD